First published in 2019 in Great Britain by
Barrington Stoke Ltd
18 Walker Street, Edinburgh, EH3 7LP

www.barringtonstoke.co.uk

Text © 2019 Keren David

A CIP catalogue record for this book is available from the British Library upon request

ISBN: 978-1-78112-855-8

Printed in China by Leo

TEEN   JUNE 2019

Renfrewshire
Council

The library is always open at
renfrewshirelibraries.co.uk

Visit now for
homework help
and free
eBooks.

We are the Skoobs and we love the library!

Phone: 0300 300 1188
Email: libraries@renfrewshire.gov.uk

*To Deborah and Jeremy, at the start of
your new adventure*

CONTENTS

1. Decisions   1

2. The Disconnect   6

3. Dad   13

4. @murraylove   18

5. Family matters   23

6. Hello FOMO   29

7. Addiction   38

8. Support group   45

9. Identity theft   51

10. Spies   59

11. Running   67

12. Choices   71

13. Info check   77

14. Snap cheat   89

15. Download   98

16. Delete and reset   106

17. Connected   109

18. Selfie   114

1
Decisions

I take a selfie.

And another.

I look awful. I can't go out like this. It's the top I'm wearing. Shaquilla can wear sexy stuff like this, but on me it just looks silly. I haven't got the body for it. I don't fill it up. It makes me look stupid. Like a kid dressing up.

I change my top to a plain white T-shirt. Apply more bronzer. Try to remember how to contour my cheekbones.

Selfie.

My lipstick's wrong. Too pink. Where's that other one?

Selfie.

OK, that'll do.

I find our group – me, Natalie, Sophie, Shaquilla. Press send.

Wait. One ... Two ... Three—

My phone buzzes with a message from Dad. Ignore it. I haven't got time right now for a long chat.

Message from Natalie: *Gorgeous as per, babe, but what is that top?*

I message back: *Just an old one of Rosa's. Not going to wear it ...*

Panic. What can I wear?

Message from Shaquilla: *What about that black one from H&M you bought last week?*

She's reading my mind. That was the one I had on first of all.

I message back: *Not sure it works.*

Messages from Shaquilla, Natalie and Sophie, all saying the same thing: *Show us!*

I pull the top on. It's too tight. It's too low cut. It's not me. I should never have bought it.

Selfie.

Oh God. Try again.

Selfie, leaning forward, looking down. Send it.

Natalie: *That's the one!*

Shaquilla: *Stunning!*

Sophie: *Yes! Babe!*

I look in the mirror. What do they see that I don't see? But three against one ... OK. It works. OK, I'll wear it.

I message: *Thanks, guys!*

Dad's FaceTiming me. I press the red button to decline.

I message Dad: *Sorry, I'm busy now. Talk later.*

Deep breaths. Find word game app. Play three rounds. Feel calmer.

I go downstairs. Mum's having breakfast, looking at her phone.

"New pictures of Zack!" Mum says, beaming. She's the proudest grandma in London.

"I know," I reply. "Rosa sent them to me too. So cute!" I'm the proudest auntie as well. It's so sad that we've never met Zack. My sister Rosa lives in New York now, which was where Zack was born – and Dad lives there too. Half my family is a whole ocean away.

"But there's another nasty review of the cafe," Mum says. "It's terrible. Avi's sure these reviews are fake. He's so worried."

Avi is my stepdad, and he and Mum opened their own cafe six months ago. It was their dream. But things aren't going to plan, and they're struggling to get customers. I try to help out as much as I can, but you can't drag people in off the street and make them eat. And even one bad review seems to scare people off.

"Oh, that's awful," I say.

Mum looks up.

"Esther!" she says. "What are you wearing?"

"It's my new top. I like it!" I try to sound as if I mean it.

"It's …" Mum begins. "You look like you're going to the beach!"

"It's a crop top, Mum."

"More like a bikini top."

"Well, I like it," I tell her. "And I'm wearing it. So you'll just have to cope with it."

"Do you really think it's suitable?" Mum asks. "I don't want old men leering at you."

"Yes, it's fine," I say, and I blow her a kiss. "I'm 16, Mum. I can choose my own clothes."

"Well, I'm not sure about it," she says. "Oh, hang on, Avi's texted me."

And Mum goes back to looking at her phone.

2

The Disconnect

On Monday at school, I can feel my phone vibrating in my pocket. It's like a wasp that's been swatted away from a jam sandwich. I'm going to have to find a way to sneak a look at it when I get out of assembly.

Ugh, what a rubbish weekend. When the girls actually saw what I looked like in that top, they sort of smirked. And a lot of pictures were taken. And now they're all over Insta, all over Snapchat. The comments will be coming in thick and fast, either fake nice or downright rude.

I should switch off my phone. That's what we're meant to do at school. But it could be something urgent. You never know. Dad likes to know he can contact me any time. And what if something happens to Rosa and Zack? I do worry about them, because they're thousands of miles away. And so is Dad, of course.

Maybe I can ease it out of my pocket ... But we're in a special assembly and someone would see. And I really can't afford to have my phone taken away.

We aren't normally called into assembly in period two. I should be doing History. The whole of Year Eleven are here. The head teacher's talking about some special guest. Must be the woman sitting next to him.

She's very smart and looks a bit scary. Her silver-blonde hair's all puffed up and she's wearing a tailored jacket and a white blouse with a floppy bow. Plus a chunky silver choker and earrings. She looks like she might be the head of Ofsted, here to close the school down. But I don't think she is, because then Mr Lamarr wouldn't be smiling, and the school would probably send letters home to our parents rather than break the news in a Year Eleven assembly. Also, the school was rated Good last time it was inspected and the sixth form got Outstanding.

"So, I'd like to welcome Dame Irene Irvine back to the school," Mr Lamarr says. "She was a pupil here back in the 1970s, and since then she's become one of our most successful former students."

Something stirs in my memory. Dame Irene Irvine. Mobile phones. Billionaire. Super impressive.

"She's got news of a very exciting new programme for you in Year Eleven," Mr Lamarr goes on, "which I hope you'll all get involved in. It's a fascinating social experiment, and I think you'll find it something that can help to improve both your exam results and your social skills ... It might even increase your happiness."

I don't know what he's going on about. It's a well-known fact that schools only care about exam results. But anyway, how can Dame Irene Irvine make us happier? Give us all free phones with unlimited data?

"Thank you, Mr Lamarr!" Dame Irene begins. "And it is so good to be back here again. I've just been treated to a tour of the grounds and I can tell you that a lot has changed since 1979! In my day, a lot of classes were taught in temporary classrooms with leaking roofs. There were no computer suites or dance studios. Even the school's name – I was a pupil at Finsbury Park Community School, not the New North London Enterprise Academy. But there's still a lot that's familiar."

I'm not interested in a history lesson, especially when I've been pulled out of a History lesson, so my mind starts wandering a bit. I think about how Natalie has gone a bit crazy about boys lately. How she likes it when they message her or like her pictures. How she's always going on at me to friend different boys. And how I find the whole thing a bit annoying but could never say so.

"So, mobile-phone technology has been my life," Dame Irene is saying. "And I am proud of what I've achieved. A few decades ago, no one could have predicted the sort of impact technology would have on our lives today."

I can't imagine a life without phones. Mum talks about it sometimes, and it just feels so strange that someone I know lived like that. It's like knowing someone who remembers Henry VIII beheading his second wife.

"Phones are a vital part of our everyday life," Dame Irene says. "We use them to communicate, to socialise, to share information and photographs, videos and links."

Typical older person with a really limited view of what phones are for. What about finding our way to places? How do you do that without GPS?

How about googling stuff? And meeting people online?

"My challenge now is to look to the future," Dame Irene continues. "What role will phones play in the decades to come? What can we do better? How can technology grow to help us even more? And that's where you come in. Year Eleven, I want you to help me."

The room buzzes with excitement. For a minute we forget to be silent and we turn to each other, words spilling out of our mouths as we try to work out what Dame Irene means. Then Ms Mohammed (head of discipline and decorum) blows her whistle and we're silent again.

"I'm creating a task force to advise me on mobile-phone culture," Dame Irene says. "And I thought there'd be no better way to recruit than by looking to *your* generation. You're digital natives. People who have grown up with this technology."

Dame Irene pauses, gazes intently at us with her piercing blue eyes, and adds, "You know more about mobile phones than I do. They've always been part of your life. You can tell me exactly what's good – and bad – about the way technology affects us. I'm sure each and every one of you could help me. But I need to find the best candidates. People who show discipline and determination. So I have a challenge for you."

A ripple of anticipation spreads across the room.

"My challenge is this," Dame Irene says. "You have to give up your mobile phone."

Every single one of us gasps in horror. Well, everyone I can see, anyway.

"The challenge will last for six weeks," Dame Irene continues, "until half term. Anyone who manages to go six weeks without their phone will win £1,000 and become a member of my task force. They'll be paid to attend meetings. Their ideas will shape the future. Those who want to take part will get simple phones, which you can use for calls and texts. You won't be out of touch in an emergency.

"I'll trust you not to cheat, and as the weaker participants drop out I'll announce ways of monitoring you further. A letter has gone to your parents today, outlining the challenge, and I'll need their permission for you to take part. I know it won't be easy. But I think and hope that we will all learn a great deal from this challenge, which I've called The Disconnect."

My brain splits into two, like it's a watermelon and Dame Irene has taken an axe to it. One half of my brain is all "My phone? My phone? She wants to take my phone away?"

But the other is "One thousand pounds! One thousand pounds! Wow! Yes, please!"

3
Dad

They're not starting the challenge immediately. At break-time, I check my phone for messages.

From Mum, telling me I'd forgotten my lunch box.

From Rosa: another super-cute video of Zack.

From Natalie: *I'm in late today, what's this special assembly, are we in trouble?*

And from Dad: *Can you FT me, Esther? Sorry about yesterday, got caught in a meeting, love you xxx*

I FaceTime Dad when I get back from school. It's 11 a.m. in New York, but he's at home today. He has a week free. You'd have thought it would have been a good time for him to come to London to visit his daughter, wouldn't you? Yes, well, I'd have thought so too.

Our conversation goes like this.

Dad (messy black hair, dark-rimmed specs, T-shirt with a picture of Bart Simpson): "Hey, Essie! Love you! How's it going?"

Me (similar hair but longer, similar specs but lighter, school uniform consisting of a white shirt, black skirt, wasp-striped yellow and black tie and the ugliest shoes in the universe): "Hey, Dad. What's up?"

Dad: "Oh, not much. Went for an audition yesterday, so fingers crossed."

Me: "Oh, good luck."

I don't bother to ask what for. Dad goes to tons of auditions but hardly ever gets picked. He's an actor, in theory, but he hasn't had an acting job in the last year. He mostly does readings and workshops and helps people develop new musicals and plays. "It'll pay off in the end," Dad always says. "Networking" is his favourite word, closely followed by "connections".

Dad: "Thanks, Essie. How's my superstar?"

Me: "Ha ha. I have no idea who that is."

Dad: "You, of course. How are you?"

Me: "I'm OK. Lots of homework. Year Eleven is a bitch."

Dad: "But you're doing OK, right? You get good grades? What did you get for that English essay?"

Dad helps me with all my homework. I do my best, then email it to him and he sends it back, all corrected and improved. Works for me. Not sure how it'll work out when I have actual exams.

Me: "Not got it back yet."

Dad: "How's your mum?"

Me: "She's fine, thanks. How's Lucille?"

Lucille is Dad's girlfriend. Sometimes she's there in the background waving at me when Dad calls. That makes me feel super self-conscious and I can't think of anything to say.

Dad: "Lucille is ..."

He scratches his head.

Dad: "She's good. Pretty good. We're good."

Me: "Glad to hear it."

Dad: "How are your friends? Natalie and Shaquilla and Sophia, is it? All well? Getting on with each other?"

Me: "It's Sophie. Yes, they're all fine."

Dad: "Essie, if there's anything bothering you, you know you can tell me, don't you? Just because I'm not there in London … I'm still your dad. I still love you."

There is stuff I could tell him. Like, money's tight, and Mum and Avi are really worried because they've sunk everything into the cafe and it's not taking off like they'd hoped. Like, I really miss Rosa. Like, I'm not so sure that I really fit in with my best friends any more, but I don't know what to do about it.

But what's the point? Dad can't do anything to help. Talking only gets you so far.

Me: "I know, Dad. Everything's good."

I blow him a kiss.

Me: "Love you! Talk to you soon!"

When the screen goes black, I realise I didn't tell Dad about The Disconnect. I didn't tell him that he won't be able to FaceTime me or send me pictures for six weeks. Well, I suppose he can, but it'll all be via Mum's laptop.

I love my dad, sure, but it's hard when you never see each other. When he lives thousands of miles away.

Our phones mean Dad and I can see each other all the time. We can talk. We can share our lives. We can be very close.

But somehow that's just not enough.

4

@murraylove

"We can do this," Natalie says. "We can so do this, babes. After all, it's only for six weeks."

Natalie is giving us a pep talk. If we're taking part in The Disconnect, we have to give our phones in tomorrow, and I'm not sure I can face it.

Nor is Sophie. "It sounded easy when Dame Irene was talking about it," Sophie says. "But … you know … it's my phone! It's a basic essential! I'd feel weird without it."

"It could be dangerous," Shaquilla adds. "If there was an emergency or something."

"We'd have the phones Dame Irene is going to give us," I point out. "We could call 999. We just wouldn't have smart phones."

"Yeah, but what if we needed information before the ambulance arrived?" Shaquilla says.

"What if someone collapses, and we need to give them mouth-to-mouth and we can't look it up on YouTube?"

"The person at ambulance control—" I start to reply, but Natalie cuts in.

"People managed this kind of stuff before smart phones were invented, Shaq. My mum's always going on about it. 'You kids, you don't know you're born. We had to have money on us and find a call box if we needed to phone home ...'"

"What's a call box?" Sophie says.

"Couldn't they just send a text?" Shaquilla asks.

"It's not about emergencies!" I burst out. "It's the everyday stuff! It's being able to talk to each other all the time! It's getting that reassurance, you know, by sending pictures ..."

"We can talk to each other at school," Natalie says. "And ... I suppose ... on our new phones."

"Yes, but that means actually talking," Shaquilla points out. "We don't do that. And we can't do that in a group."

Nat's laughing. "Of course we can do that. We're doing it now!"

"Yes, but … it's different," Shaquilla says.

She's right. The new phones hardly count. Old-style technology just won't give us the chance to communicate properly, and in order to talk face to face as a group, we'd need to be in the same place at the same time, which isn't very likely.

I'm a member of about 25 different groups on various apps. Some groups are small – like me and Nat, for when Shaq and Sophie wind us up. Me and Sophie and Shaq, for when Nat's being annoying. My English group. My mates from primary school – except Lucy, because she upset Natalie once and there was a massive row and a split. Lucy's group from that time. Natalie's group from that time … The groups aren't always active, but it's a way of making sure you don't upset the wrong people, while knowing everything that's going on.

And then there's all the stuff on my phone that I do to stay calm. Meditation apps. Mindfulness apps. Word games. Films and Netflix and magazines and … kitten videos. Sometimes a cute cat is what you need after an upsetting day. What would it be like if you couldn't get instant access to YouTube?

"I'm feeling all shaky just thinking about it," I confess. "But I'd love to win the money."

"How rich must Dame Irene be?" Shaquilla says. "I mean, there could be a hundred of us that make it to six weeks and then she'd be forking out a fortune."

"She's a billionaire," Natalie says. "I looked her up."

"On your phone ..." Shaquilla adds, giving Natalie the side-eye.

"No, on Mum's laptop," Natalie tells her.

"We could use laptops to make up for not having phones," I say.

"Esther, all the messaging apps are on our phones," Sophie points out. "I mean, I suppose you could go back to Facebook ..."

We all groan.

"Yeah, if you want your gran and your aunties and everyone knowing your business," Shaquilla says.

"But let's face it, it's not going to be the same," Sophie says. "And anyway, if we all give up our phones, who are we going to be talking to?"

"Well …" I say. There's a whole group of people on Twitter I know because I'm a fan of Murray Myles (I'm @murraylove – but none of my friends know). And then there are the people I did ballet with for years, until I broke my ankle and had to give up. And then Rosa … Dad …

"I hate this," I say, feeling miserable.

"Think of the money!" Natalie tells me. "What would you buy? I'd go on a massive shopping trip to Westfield, and I'd get eyelash extensions …"

And there it is. The reason I have to do this. The reason why it's worth the sacrifice.

"I would go to New York," I say. "I'd take Mum. So we can see my sister and her baby."

"And your dad," Sophie says.

"Yeah," I answer. "Him too."

5
Family matters

My family's kind of complicated, as you've probably realised.

My dad is American and my mum is British. They met in New York when Mum was a student on a year abroad. They got together and had Rosa. It was all pretty quick.

After a few years, Mum got really homesick and they came back to London, where they got married and I was born. Dad came to the UK on a student visa and he did a course in musical theatre. And then he taught for a bit and got some acting work. But Mum and Dad didn't have much money, and Dad didn't have a work visa.

And all of that stress meant a lot of arguments, and in the end they split up and Dad went back to America. His visa had run out anyway, so he couldn't live here any longer.

Dad went back to New York. And he's still an actor and he's done plays and musicals, but he's never really made it big. His name is Don Levin. If you saw that Netflix thing about the aliens and the rock band, he played the bus driver.

Most of the time Dad works as a helper in a centre for disabled kids. He's really good at it, and everyone loves him – but it doesn't pay very well.

Mum brought me and Rosa up on her own and Dad sent money when he could. He'd fly over to see us whenever he could afford to. Which wasn't very often. I've been to New York twice. Once when I was six and Dad had a small part in a Broadway musical – Rosa, Mum and I went to see him. And when I was 12, Rosa and I went to see our American grandma, who was sick. She died while we were out there. It wasn't the most fun week, obviously, but it was good to be able to support Dad when he was so sad, and not just pretend-hug him on the phone.

Anyway, when Rosa went to uni, she picked a course which had a year in New York – just like Mum had. I was so jealous of Rosa being there and hanging out with Dad a lot. Like, I'm really close to Mum, and Avi's a great stepdad, but I've never spent a long time with Dad and I'd love to have that connection. I've never had it. It must be so different face to face, not face to FaceTime.

Rosa loved New York so much that she went back after she finished her degree. And she met Carlos. And about a month later she got pregnant with Zack.

It wasn't the best way to start a relationship, and no one knew that more than Rosa. It was very similar to how Mum and Dad got together. And that didn't work out so well.

So now my family is split in half. Dad and Rosa and baby Zack are in America. Mum and Avi and I are in London. I have stepbrothers and sisters too, Avi's kids, but they are all grown up and they live in Israel, where Avi's from. Like I said, it's complicated.

"So, I have to give up my phone," I'm explaining to Rosa on FaceTime, "because of this thing called The Disconnect. But it's just for six weeks and then I'll have £1,000. If I put it together with everything I've saved from babysitting, then maybe I can buy flights for Mum and me to come out and see you."

Zack is gurgling at me on the screen. He is the cutest baby. He has huge chocolate-brown eyes and tight curls and about five chins. I'd love to be able to kiss his dimples, breathe in his baby smell.

"Whoa," Rosa says. "What is this experiment? Sounds extreme."

I explain the rules. And Rosa points out that we can still Skype in the evenings on Mum's laptop, and she'll email pictures of Zack and it'll all be fine.

But I know that I'll miss our random messages and sending photos back and forth. I won't have that feeling that, while half of my family might be thousands of miles away, they're still with me all the time. In my pocket.

"It'll be OK," Rosa says. "Look, I'll go out and buy stamps and postcards, and you can too, and we can send them to each other. Just like Mum did with her sister when I was a baby."

We still have those postcards. Mum must have sent about a hundred to Auntie Tamsin, and Auntie Tamsin sent the same number back. When Auntie Tamsin died from heart problems, her partner gave the postcards back to Mum. She put them all together and stuck them in a bag and said, "I must do something with these sometime." They've been in her cupboard ever since.

Rosa and I read all the postcards a few years back, hungrily searching for clues about why our parents' love story went wrong. But we didn't find much. It's hard to read between the lines when the lines say "New York is wonderful" and "I can't tell you how happy I am with Don and Rosa in our cute apartment. Even the smell of Mexican food from the cafe downstairs feels exotic and exciting."

"Yeah," I say to Rosa now. "We can do the postcard thing."

"Have you told Dad about it?" Rosa asks.

I shrug and say, "No, can you?" She rolls her eyes and tells me that I really should tell him myself.

"I know," I say. "But he'll want to talk it over and, you know ..."

Sometimes it's good having a screen dad. I get a lot of attention when we're talking. It's all very face to face.

But sometimes I'd like the chance to tell Dad stuff just casually. To have him in the background being annoying – like most people's dads.

Anyway, just then Zack starts crying and Rosa has to go. I switch off my phone for a bit to see how I'll feel during The Disconnect.

And how I feel is bored and anxious and lonely, so I switch it right back on again.

6
Hello FOMO

Today's the day. Disconnect day. We have to give in our phones.

"It's not a bad idea at all," Mum says. "You'll be able to focus more on your homework. And perhaps you'll have more time to help out in the cafe?"

"I can, but do you actually need my help?" I ask her.

"You never know when you might need an extra pair of hands," Mum says. "It got quite busy yesterday. We had three family groups in, and then a couple ordered the falafel plate ... It was the busiest day we've had for ages. Maybe things are on the turn."

I hope so.

Mum and Avi set up the cafe a year ago. They'd planned it for ages. Middle Eastern flavours with an English twist. At first things went really well. But then some random person left a stinking review on TripAdvisor and it changed everything.

"The review wouldn't have mattered so much if the cafe had been open longer," Avi says. A lot.

"I just don't understand it," Mum always replies. "How can someone hate our scrambled egg with hummus and beetroot?"

They've both got a bit obsessed with the bad review. Avi even played back the footage from the security camera to try to work out who'd left it.

"It will change," I tell Mum. "The food is amazing." I take my plate to the sink and wash it up.

"You'll hardly notice not having your phone," Mum says. "After all, everyone's in the same boat! No one will have their phones, so you can all support each other. And I do worry about you walking around with your phone in your hand. You hear all these reports about moped muggers ..."

"Yeah, right," I say.

"Maybe you'll actually talk to people! You might make some new friends."

"Ha ha," I say. "Very funny. Perhaps you should try it too."

Then I pick up my bag. I can't put it off any longer. Time for school.

When I get there, the playground is full of small knots of Year Elevens shouting at each other. Seems like my group of friends weren't the only ones debating The Disconnect.

"I'm not doing it!" Saira Shah is saying to her mates. "I don't need some sort of bribe to get me to control my phone use. And I don't want to be that dame's advisor anyway."

"I can't," Evie Lennox moans to the netball team. "How can I count my steps and monitor my fitness without my phone? I can't buy myself a Fitbit just for six weeks."

Natalie appears at my side and asks, "Done it yet?" She waves an old-fashioned, tiny non-smart phone at me. "I have! Come on, I'll take you."

She hustles me across the playground towards Mr Lamarr's office.

"They're doing it here," Natalie says. "You give your phone to Miss Chen." She nods at Mr Lamarr's secretary. "And then she labels it and puts it in a bag. And you have to sign a contract ..." Natalie picks up a piece of paper. "And then they give you your new phone. First thing you have to do is call your mum so she has your new number."

I feel like I'm in a dream – or a nightmare – as I hand my phone over. What am I doing? Why am I doing this? Can I really disconnect myself from my family ... from my life ...?

"You wouldn't believe the drama I've seen this morning!" Miss Chen says as she puts my phone into a plastic bag. "Girls in tears! Boys dithering, changing their minds ..."

I can't help noticing that there are a lot of non-smart phones left in the box.

"I thought everyone had to hand in their phones before first period?" I ask.

"Hmm, yes," Miss Chen says. "Take-up has been a bit disappointing. It was voluntary after all. Maybe your generation just can't imagine giving up their phones for even six weeks."

Miss Chen hands me my new phone. I hate it right away. It's so tinny. So tiny. So black and white. So lacking in everything that makes a phone a phone.

"Ugh," I say. "What's my new number?"

She finds her list. Writes my name. Shows me the number and ... I see on the list that only 71 people have signed up for The Disconnect. Out of 300! I'm number 72.

"Hang on ..." I say. I look at the clock on Miss Chen's wall. (How will I be able to tell the time without my phone?) There's only five minutes to first period.

"No one's doing it!" I whisper to Natalie. "Everyone else will be messaging and we'll be missing out!"

Natalie's scribbling down my new number.

"It'll be fine," she tells me. "Don't worry. Thanks, miss!"

Natalie leads me out into the corridor. The empty corridor.

"Nat, what the hell?" I say. "No one's doing this!"

"Loads of people are!" she says, trying to reassure me.

"What about Shaquilla and Sophie? Where are they?"

Natalie pauses. And then two boys pass us and go into Miss Chen's room.

River Jones. And Tommy Olivero.

Tommy Olivero. Snake hips, dazzling teeth (his mum's an orthodontist), glossy chestnut hair (his dad's a hairdresser) that tumbles over his blue eyes. He's clever too, but not swotty at all. He's posh (he lives in a massive house just off the High Street), funny, enigmatic (he has three friends and only really talks to them). The rumour is that he has a girlfriend at St Clare's, the private school nearby.

I've never spoken to Tommy, unless you count the time he asked me what the French word for biscuit was. We were in a French lesson, so that's not weird at all.

Then there's River Jones. River used to be a bit of a pain – you could never believe a word he said. He just made up stupid stories about everything.

But last year that changed. It turned out there was some amazing but true story about his dad being an undercover policeman, and his mum was on the news. River went a bit sad and didn't talk much. I've always wanted to ask him more about what happened, but we don't have any classes together so I haven't. Yet.

"OK, so Shaquilla and Sophie sort of changed their minds," Natalie says. "But that's good, because they can tell us everything that's going on."

"What? When did they change their minds?" I ask. "Why didn't anyone tell me?"

"They were talking about it yesterday and I tried to persuade them," Natalie says.

I've been without my phone for two minutes and already my fear of missing out – FOMO, Rosa calls it – is at emergency levels.

"They didn't even tell me!" I say. I'm wondering why I wasn't part of this conversation. Have Natalie and Sophie and Shaquilla got a group that doesn't include me?

"They said Dina Mubarak set up some sort of group to boycott The Disconnect," Nat explains.

"She did some really intensive lobbying and so loads of people decided not to bother."

Dina used to sit next to me in Maths in Year Eight, and we got on really well. OK, so we haven't really spoken in person for more than a year, but then who does? I mean, we never fell out. We're in some of the same groups. I wouldn't expect her to ignore my existence completely ...

"I don't care," I say as I try to blink back the stupid tears that have sprung into my eyes. "I can do this. Who cares about a stupid phone, anyway? I'd rather have the money."

"Exactly!" says Tommy Olivero, who's just come out of Miss Chen's office. "I was just telling River here, people are weak. They're addicted. They can't cope without their electronic drug."

River's nodding and adds, "I've been meaning to go off-grid for ages. These apps, these social media companies, they just use you. They spy on you. They gather your data and sell it, and try to sell stuff to you. It's really sinister."

River is deadly serious.

"But aren't we just being used by Dame Irene for her research?" I ask. "Isn't she going to use us to sell even more mobile phones?"

"Hmm, interesting question," River says. "I'm going to have to think about it. I guess this will give me more headspace."

"We should set up a support group," Natalie says. "We can help each other during these six weeks."

She's making a lot of eye contact with Tommy Olivero. He gives her a flash of his perfect teeth.

"Good idea," Tommy says. "Where and when?"

Natalie opens her mouth. But I get in first.

"My parents have a cafe," I say. "It's called Basabousa. It's on Stroud Green Road, just past Sainsbury's. How about there on Friday?"

7
Addiction

I can't do this.

I really can't.

I just need to check my phone … I just need to check … I just need …

I can't do this.

"Finding it difficult without a phone?" Avi asks me on day two. I've done my homework in the cafe, where he's served me hummus and *malawach*, which is the most delicious flatbread imaginable – all puffy and buttery. Now I'm cutting peppers for Avi to make the sauce that goes with *shashouka*. If you've never had it, it's the absolute best way to eat eggs – like a spicy tomato soup with floating poached eggs.

"Really difficult," I tell him. "Like, impossible. I feel really twitchy, and I can't focus on anything."

"Why don't you get together with your friends?" Avi asks. "Go to the park?"

"It's raining. And also, how would I get in touch with them?"

"They all have phones like you do, don't they?"

"I don't know their numbers," I moan.

"Well, get their numbers," Avi tells me. "Or go and see them. Everyone lives near here, don't they?"

"You can't just go round to someone's house!" I say. "You have to be asked!"

Avi shakes his head. "I don't understand kids today. When I was a kid, we just all hung out at the beach."

I give up trying to explain to Avi why London today is different to Tel Aviv in the 1970s. And not only because we don't have a beach.

My phone rings. I jab at the button to answer it, hating its tinny ringtone.

"Hey!" Natalie says. "You'll never guess what."

It's so weird to hear her voice crackling out of a phone. We *always* message. We never even FaceTime. We're both self-conscious about our voices.

"Well, I'm round at Shaquilla's—"

"What?" I interrupt Natalie. "How come she didn't ask me?"

"We just did last period together and she mentioned it," Natalie says. "Don't think she's got your number, babe."

Maybe not, I think, *but you have.*

"Anyway, all sorts of stuff is going down," Natalie continues. "And we have no idea about any of it."

I know Natalie's a bit of a drama queen. But still …

"After two days?" I say.

And she's off. How this one is fancying that one and that one is angry with this one, and Nancy's set up a group for her party, and Shaquilla's in it but Sophie isn't, and what about us?

"We won't be invited to anything for six weeks," I say, and my heart sinks a bit.

"I know, babe," Natalie says. "Anyway, get yourself down here. You're missing out."

But I say no. It's a bit late to go all the way to Shaquilla's now – she lives down near the Arsenal stadium. And I need to finish the peppers for Avi.

Avi and Mum met five years ago. They're perfect for each other. They have so much in common. They both love to cook and sing. They love walking in the countryside, going to see movies and reading the *Guardian*. Mum had been internet dating a bit before they met, but without any success. "Who wants to meet a single mum in her forties?" Mum would ask. Then she went to dinner at a friend's house, met Avi, and they talked and talked and talked. He was a single parent, so they had that in common.

Mum said it was an instant connection, but I think it was something that started because they had a lot to talk about, and then bit by bit they found out all the other things they shared. They're both very honest. They both believe in sticking up for people who haven't had great chances in life. They're passionate about education – Mum's at her Japanese evening class right now, and Avi's learning to code. They both have friends from all over. And luckily Rosa and I love Avi too.

Anyway, a year after Mum and Avi met, he moved in, and a year after that they opened Basabousa.

He's so different from my dad. Avi's bald, with a handlebar moustache. He's short and solid, and he doesn't talk much because English is his fifth language. He's practical. He makes things. And this cafe means the world to him because he's made every bit of it, from painting the walls a shade of Mediterranean turquoise, to creating a menu made up mostly of the foods he ate when he was growing up – Yemeni, Moroccan, Egyptian and Israeli flavours. "This place, it is me," Avi always says. "It is my family. It is my past, our present, our future."

I liked Avi as soon as Mum introduced us. I'd never say this to anyone, but sometimes I wish he was my real dad. And now he's looking at me, his head on one side, his eyes all twinkly.

"Go and meet your friends," Avi says. "It's OK. I can manage. We're not exactly rushed off our feet in here."

"No, I don't want to." I'm not sure I can explain it, but I have a go. "They'll just be talking about stuff on their phones. And I want to see what happens without a phone. I want to see what life's like without one."

Avi shrugs. "Whatever you want, princess."

"And I've got a postcard to write for Rosa," I tell him. "I got stamps on the way home from school."

I pull the postcard out. It was kind of difficult to find one, because Finsbury Park isn't exactly a part of London that tourists visit – it's all people and shops and traffic, and even the park's a bit scruffy. Maybe I'll go into central London at the weekend to buy more. This postcard was tucked into a corner of our local newsagent's, left over from the last royal wedding. There's a smudge on the prince's nose. Never mind. Rosa knows what he looks like.

I finish the peppers and Avi pours hot water over fresh mint in a tall glass. I take the drink and my postcard to the window table. I chew my pen a bit and then I write:

Dear Rosa,

It feels so weird actually writing to you, with a pen, and knowing you won't get this for ages. Like I've time-travelled to the past. I wish you were here, you and Zack, in Basabousa, drinking mint tea (not great for Zack, I know, but one day!).

We could think up a way to get more customers, because it's so sad that Mum and Avi work so hard and no one comes. The food is so good.

I've hardly started, but I've run out of space. So I squeeze *Love you lots, Esther xxxxxxxxxxxxxx PS Love to Dad* into the last corner.

Next time I'll make my writing a lot smaller.

8

Support group

The week really drags, but at last it's Friday and here we are at Basabousa. There are ten of us crowded round a table – the Disconnect support group. I think we must make up about a quarter of the kids who are still taking part in The Disconnect, because there are a lot fewer than at the start. All week, people have been going to Miss Chen's office to get their phones back.

The latest one was Marcus O'Malley. He ran round the playground yesterday, followed by a cheering crowd, holding his iPhone in his hand like it was the Olympic flame. Loads of people were taking pictures and – according to Shaquilla and Sophie – posting them on Instagram.

In fact, according to Sophie I was in one of those pictures, and it wasn't very flattering. "I'll tell you who wrote the nasty comments about you, if you want," Sophie said at school earlier.

I felt sick and somehow ashamed that I couldn't see for myself. Why, I don't know.

"I think they're taking a liberty," Sophie added. "They know they're going behind your back."

"You could look yourself later," Shaquilla said. "If you won't look at my phone, you can use your mum's laptop."

"But she can't comment, so what's the point?" Natalie said. "You speak up for her. You're meant to be her friend."

"I really don't care," I told them, and tried to look completely unbothered. "When you come off social media, you realise how stupid it is."

"Yes, I agree," Natalie said. But I could see Shaquilla and Sophie weren't so sure. I wish they'd ditched their phones too. Now it's like we're speaking different languages.

Anyway, never mind them. Here we are – the support group – drinking Mum's homemade pink lemonade and eating Basabousa cake. It's Avi's Yemenite grandmother's recipe. The cake is soaked in syrup and flavoured with orange blossom water and is just delicious. Everyone in the support group thinks so too, judging by the speed with which it's wolfed down. So Avi brings out a plate of ka'ak cookies stuffed with dates and then disappears into the kitchen.

"Wow," River says, brushing away the crumbs. "This is great, Esther."

"Thanks," I say.

I'm about to suggest that if everyone likes the food they should tell their families to come here, but River thumps on the table and says, "OK! Shut up! How's it going?"

A babble of noise. Everyone's complaining.

"OK, how about this?" River asks. "Is anyone actually enjoying not having a phone?"

Silence. And then a girl speaks up. Her voice is so soft that we have to lean towards her to hear.

"I didn't have a smart phone to start with. I don't like them. So I had to persuade Dame Irene to let me be part of The Disconnect. I mean, I wasn't really disconnecting from anything."

"Is that even fair?" Natalie blurts out, but everyone shushes her.

"I had a smart phone until last year, but I didn't like it," the girl says. "I found it really stressful. I was always worrying about saying the right thing and being in the right groups."

I know this girl, just a bit. She's in my Geography class. She was in my English class last year. But I can't remember her name. I don't know anything about her.

"And then," the girl continues, "my friends started being mean to me. I don't know why. They'd talk about parties and things but never tell me the details. And then afterwards they'd put the pictures on the group chat and act all surprised if I asked them why I wasn't included. I mean, I began to feel a bit paranoid. I was checking my phone the whole time."

Maura. That's her name. Maura.

"And then the nasty comments started," Maura goes on. "I'd post a picture and they'd just ..." She looks down at her hands. "Well, I don't want to go over the whole thing again. Put it this way, I got rid of my phone. It gave them power over me, and I took that power back."

"And did they stop?" I ask.

"How would she know?" Natalie snaps.

Maura shrugs. "True, I don't know. I'm not on social media. I don't do any of that. I keep offline. It's quieter. I found it hard at first, but now … I don't know … I can focus better. Everything doesn't have to be instant."

"But have you actually got any friends?" Natalie asks. I think she realises as soon as she's said it that she's been way too blunt, because she's looking at her nail varnish and not making eye contact with Maura. Meanwhile, Maura blushes and blinks her eyes a bit.

"Natalie doesn't mean it like that," I say. "She means, isn't it hard to keep up with people's plans and stuff?"

Maura shakes her head. "To be honest, I don't have many friends. My friends are outside school – my cousins, my neighbours. I do feel left out. And sometimes it feels like people are talking about me behind my back, and that just makes me want to disappear altogether."

Maura's totally crying now. The girl next to her puts her arm round Maura.

"I'm so sorry," the girl says. "I had no idea."

"None of us did," I say. "This is horrible, Maura. But now we can all be your friends. After all, we're all in the same position."

Maura manages a small wobbly smile and says, "I was so excited when The Disconnect was announced. I thought, this could really change things."

"It could," the girl next to her says. Hannah, she's called. I remember she had a really cool Instagram account featuring her cute pug.

"And you know, it's not all bad," Maura says. "I read more. I cook. I did a course over the summer in bicycle maintenance, which was kind of cool …"

It all sounds a bit lame, but everyone's nodding like Maura's a guru who's leading us to a different, cleaner, slower sort of life.

"And my grades have gone up massively," Maura adds.

9
Identity theft

River talks next. He's got a whole speech prepared.

He quotes statistics. He talks about mental health. Lack of focus. Poor social skills.

River tells us all about how social media companies misuse our data. How we're just pawns in the hands of people making money out of us. How identity thieves can use our information to steal from us.

"You know those stupid quizzes?" River says. "Which Harry Potter character are you? Well, they just use all that to find out more about you. And those things like your film-star name, your porn-star name, the name of your first pet plus your grandmother's surname? They are designed to find out your passwords. We're all just mugs. We're handing ourselves over to the enemy."

River is very passionate, but he does go on a bit. In the end, a murmur of conversation starts buzzing in the background and River's speech stumbles to a halt.

Natalie's been whispering into Tommy Olivero's ear for at least five minutes. "Well, that was all fascinating," Natalie says, "but I've got to go. Thanks for the cake and lemonade, Esther."

She sounds a bit snarky. Was it babyish, serving lemonade? Should I have had the group round to the flat for crisps and cider?

Everyone goes. All apart from River. He's looking pretty downcast.

"I don't think anyone gets it," he says.

"I think everyone got a bit confused. All that stuff about data mining, it's quite complicated," I tell him.

River runs his hands through his hair. He's got nice hair, I think, all springy and wild. He's grown it a lot in the last year. He's taller too. And he's much more serious.

"Just because something's complicated doesn't mean it's not worth listening to," River says.

"I know that," I reply.

"Weren't they listening when I told them how phones mean you can't focus?" he asks.

"Maybe they're still affected," I say. "I thought what you were saying was very interesting, but I did find myself wishing I could video it." He looks baffled, so I add, "Then I could have shared it."

"Really?" River says, and there's this slightly awkward moment where I swear he's blushing. I can't think of anything to say that won't add to the idea that I have a crush on him. Which I don't, but I'm guessing I might have given that impression.

"There are people out there who steal other people's identities," River continues. "And we make it easy for them." He pauses. "Look, Esther, you might not know this, but my dad … my real dad … I never knew him. He stole someone else's identity. He took this false name, and he spied on my mum and her friends …"

"Why?" I ask him.

"Mum was an environmental activist, and he was a policeman. An undercover cop. And it all went too far and he ended up in a relationship with my mum. Do you know what that does to you? What it did to her?"

"It must have been awful," I answer.

"Yeah. It was. And now we're just handing over our information, in the most stupid way possible, to anyone. We don't have the first idea of what they will do with it."

I don't know what to say. "I'm so sorry. I never realised. I don't do those personality tests." (I gave them up when I did one and it said that my dream lover was Murray Myles from Sun Fixation. Which was spot on, actually, but my secret. Natalie teased me for days, and I felt totally embarrassed and had to say nasty things about Murray to shut her up. Which was annoying for several reasons.)

River smiles. He's got a great smile. His face is quite thin and his mouth is big, and so his grin takes up all of the bottom of his face. It's impossible to look at and not smile as well.

"It's really messed up my head, you know?" River says. "It's hard to explain to people with normal families."

"I've not exactly got a normal family," I say. "I never lived with my dad." River looks puzzled, so I explain that Avi is my stepdad. (He's still in the kitchen, chopping parsley to make salads and looking all hopeful because the cafe has two bookings tonight.) "My real dad lives in America. But he hasn't got any money, and nor do we, so we never see him. I mean, we FaceTime a lot, except now we have to Skype, because of the no phone thing ..."

"Ugh, that's hard," River says.

"It'd feel weird to spend time with Dad now," I say. "I'm used to it."

River's watching me. "But you're not happy about it, are you?"

I try to smile. "It's OK. It's just pretty full on, you know? Like we can't just be around each other, watching TV or whatever. We have to have important conversations all the time. Sometimes I can't think of anything to say."

"I can imagine that," River says. "I don't ever want to talk to my real dad. Good thing we've got stepdads, eh?"

"Yes," I nod, even though I think our situations are very different. No one would want to talk to a dad like River's. My dad is lovely. It's just that I never get to hug him. And sometimes I feel sad that being in New York seems to be more important to him than being with me, even if he and Mum both say it isn't like that.

"Are you finding it really difficult, not having your phone?" I ask. "Because I am."

"I'm surprised," he says. "I'm liking it. It gives me more space to think. And be. I've been running a lot. And doing research. And reading."

"I like reading," I tell him. And it's true, books have helped a bit. I don't feel so twitchy when I'm wrapped up in a book. I'm not thinking about what I'm missing out on. Last night I read for two hours before I went to bed. I haven't done that for years. I fell asleep right away. Normally it takes me ages to drop off.

"I don't think I'll go back to having a smart phone," River says. "I don't want to be on social media. But I want to campaign ... about data mining and other stuff. How can I do that without social media?"

"There must be ways." I try to think. "You could write letters to people? Protest? Go and see your MP?"

"I'm keeping a diary about The Disconnect," he says. "Jason – that's my stepdad – is a journalist, and he thinks maybe I can write an article about it. About our experiences. About Dame Irene."

"Dame Irene?" I ask.

"Well, it is a bit weird, isn't it?" River says. "Why is Dame Irene taking phones away from us? She makes the things."

It is weird. I hadn't really thought about it before.

River shakes his head. "We need to find out more about her."

"I'll help if you want," I say. "I need things to do now so I'm not thinking about my phone all the time."

"Thanks," River says. "Do you want to come running sometime?"

When he leaves, I feel like I've made a new friend. Several new friends, actually. I'm going to look out for Maura and some of the others at school.

I get out one of the other postcards that I bought to send to Rosa and I write on it:

Hey Rosa,

The experiment is going OK. It's hard, but I have more time for things like reading. And I'm making different friends, or I think so anyway, and might be going running. Life feels slower and sort of cleaner, if that makes sense. Or clearer, anyway. But it's a bit strange. Like when you fly on a plane and your ears go funny and you can't hear properly? My life is muffled.

Not that I get to go on planes much, but maybe this will change that! Hopefully I'll win the £1,000 so I can come to New York!

Did you get my first card? Have you sent me any cards? Did you explain The Disconnect to Dad? Send him my love.

Miss you.
Esther xxxxxxx

10
Spies

I get my first postcard from Rosa the next Monday. On one side is a picture of the Statue of Liberty. On the other she's written:

Dear Essie,

Love you and miss you loads. Looking forward to getting your first card and maybe Skyping soon. Zack misses your face on our phone! Dad's babysitting tonight and Carlos and I are going out. First date since Z was born! Squeezing into my black dress.

Love, love, love you, little sis xxxxxx

PS You are brave Disconnecting. Wish I could.

I love it. I love it so much that I burst into tears over breakfast and Mum offers me her phone to FaceTime Rosa. Luckily, we realise it'd be too early for her. "It's not really cheating, is it?" Mum asks. "It's my phone and my account."

I dither. "It's not strictly cheating, but it is cheating," I say. "I mean, I wouldn't feel good about it. And I think it'd make The Disconnect harder."

"I remember when I gave up sugar," Mum says. "It was hell for a fortnight and then I felt better than I ever had. And I lost two stone so easily."

"So why didn't you keep off it?" I ask.

"I wanted to," Mum says as she spreads marmalade on her toast. "And then I made an exception for our wedding cake. And then it was my birthday, and then ... well, I love marmalade. And cakes. And now I run a cafe. It was just too hard."

"Hmm," I say. "I'd better be going. Don't want to be late for school. Maybe we can Skype Rosa later."

"And your dad," Mum says.

At lunch-time, I remember Maura and look around for her. She's sitting on her own in a far corner of the playground, eating a sandwich and reading a book. I nudge Natalie.

"Look, Maura," I say. "All on her own."

"So what?" Natalie says.

"Well, couldn't we go and keep her company?" I suggest.

"What and hear more about life without a smart phone?" Natalie moans. "Listen, Esther, don't go weird on me here. We're doing this to get money and buy better phones, OK? And clothes and make-up and stuff."

"And a ticket to New York," I remind her.

"That Maura shouldn't even be allowed to take part in The Disconnect," Natalie says. "She said it herself. She's got nothing to disconnect from."

"She seemed really nice though," I say. "And a bit lonely."

"Well, you go if you want to. I'm going to talk to Tommy. Look, River's with him."

There is no way that I'm going over there with Natalie, who's so keen on Tommy that it's a bit embarrassing. Also, I'm kind of annoyed that she thinks she can give me permission to spend time with Maura. I make my own decisions.

"OK," I say to Natalie. "Say hi from me." And before she can reply, I'm walking towards Maura. I can imagine Nat's face – her eyes, like lasers, shooting holes in my back.

It's not that Natalie's very bossy or I'm especially quiet. It's just that we've been friends since we were nine, and Natalie is the sort of person that you keep being friends with because you hear what she says about her enemies.

Not seeing Natalie online, not seeing her comments – it's been a relief. And I've managed fine without taking six pictures of myself every day to send to her for approval before I leave the house.

In fact, maybe I'd rather stay Disconnected from Natalie for longer than six weeks.

By the time I reach Maura and sit down next to her, Natalie's with Tommy and River. She's laughing, touching River's arm, glancing over at me. I refuse to imagine what she's saying.

"Hey," I say to Maura. "Hope you don't mind me sitting here."

"Not at all," she says. "Thanks for Friday. I love your cafe."

"Oh well, it's my mum and stepdad's, not mine. It was nice to see it full of people."

"Isn't it normally?" Maura asks.

I explain about the toxic review.

"I can tell people about it," says Maura, "like my parents. And my grandparents."

"Thanks, Maura," I say.

"And couldn't you advertise?"

"They tried that," I tell her. "But I think people look the cafe up online first."

"Annoying," she says. "I'll think about it. I'm sure there must be a way. How are you coping without a phone? What's the worst thing?"

I explain about Rosa and Zack and Dad in New York, and she sympathises. I tell her about the postcards, and she says she knows a good shop for cards, just up the road in Stroud Green, and maybe we could go there together after school. Then the bell goes and we walk across the playground together. She seems like such a nice girl. And she lives fairly near us, just over the other side of the park.

We're going into the side entrance, by the school hall, when we see a woman coming towards us. Black trouser suit. Clipboard. White hair. Pearl earrings. Dame Irene Irvine is visiting again.

"Hello, girls," Dame Irene says, stopping in front of us. "Coming to the hall?"

"Err … I've got Maths," I say.

"But you're part of the Disconnect programme, aren't you?" Dame Irene asks, and bares her dazzling white teeth. "Emma … no, Esther …"

I'm stunned that she knows my name.

"Yes, but—"

"We're monitoring you all very closely," Dame Irene says. Her smile is like a shark that's spotted a tasty shoal of mackerel. "How's it going, dear?"

"Err, OK," I say. "But I really have got Maths."

But then River and Natalie and Tommy appear, and it turns out that we have all been told to go to the hall. "See you there," Dame Irene says, and she trots off down the corridor.

We sit in a row, and I'm in prime position to notice that Natalie and Tommy keep bumping knees. River, on my other side, has used aftershave, which he certainly didn't do when I sat next to him in Year Seven – back when he used to pretend that he was a champion sky-diver descended from Saxon royalty. Then I thought he was strange. Now, as River turns and smiles at me, I'm thinking that I'm glad we're friends. And I'm glad he's still in The Disconnect, because not many other people are. Maybe forty of us in total, all crammed into the first few rows in the hall.

Mr Lamarr says a few words, mostly along the lines of well done, keep going, stay strong. Then Dame Irene shimmers onto the stage. She's not smiling any more.

"Well," Dame Irene says. "How interesting. You are the strong ones. You are the ones who are not scared to go against the flow. You are the outliers. You are the mavericks."

"The what?" Natalie whispers to me.

"We're weird," I whisper back.

"You aren't scared of standing out from the crowd," Dame Irene continues. "You're bold and independent and strong."

I'm getting bored. We've got a Maths exam coming up and I can't afford to miss a lesson to listen to this.

Dame Irene gets to the point.

"But it wouldn't be fair if some of you were cheating," she says. "So, we're asking you to keep an eye on each other. Is anyone bending the rules? From now on, no borrowing phones from friends or family. No use at all of social media accounts. We'll be monitoring you, and you'll be monitoring each other. And if you report someone and it's proven they were cheating … Well, their £1,000 goes to you."

11
Running

It's 7 a.m. on Saturday morning and River and I are heading for the park. I'm a bit self-conscious in shorts and a T-shirt, but Mum assured me I looked fine, saying, "And anyway, you're going running. Not to a fashion show."

Not for the first time, I wish that Rosa still lived with us. And I actually wish I'd been able to take a selfie and send it for Natalie's approval – except then she'd know what I was doing. And there's something a bit exciting about not having told any of my friends what I've got planned.

Who'd have thought I could be so secretive? Or is this just what privacy means?

We get to the park and walk up to the bit with the cafe and the loos and the playground, because River thinks it's best to run downhill first, to warm up. "Twice round the perimeter is 5k," River says, "but if you've never run before, that might be a bit much for you."

"I've run a bit, but not for ages," I tell him.

Why not? I used to be busy all the time. But now I realise that a lot of being busy involved keeping up with stuff on my phone. And also, running was something that Rosa and I did together. And she's not here any more.

We start off down the hill. The weather is perfect – not too hot, but not cold at all, a little breeze, a bit of sunshine sparkling on the lake. There are geese and ducks, crows and gulls crying from the trees. And I'm remembering how good it feels to be running – to feel alive from my head to my toes. To feel that my whole body is doing something, not just my head or my eyes or ears.

We round the corner and jog on to the part of the park that Rosa calls the ugly bit, but I like it because it's a wide avenue lined with trees. You can hear traffic and you can see buses and buildings, and you know you're part of a big city heaving with people, but you've found a little bit of peace and space for yourself.

And then we're climbing up the steepest part of the hill again to take us back to where we started.

"Phew!" I say. I'm tired but up for another lap. This time we go slower, and at the end I slow to a walk, but River's impressed.

"It won't take you long," he tells me. "You'll be back doing 5k really soon."

I'm sure my face must be bright red, and I can feel sweat trickling down the back of my neck. I must look awful. But I don't really care. River is looking pretty sweaty himself.

"I didn't think you'd be that good," he says.

"Why not?"

"I don't know, I never saw you as sporty."

"I don't like school sport really," I tell him. "I don't like competitions, teams, that sort of thing. It makes me worried about letting people down." I have a flashback to the Year Five netball tournament. I threw the ball to the wrong person and Natalie refused to talk to me for what felt like a month.

"I used to be into football," River says. "But then things went a bit crazy in my life and I stopped. Maybe I should start again."

We go and get water from the cafe and then wander along the path that runs down the middle of the park. Then, suddenly, River stops dead.

"What is it?" I ask him.

"There – look – on that bench," he says.

River points, and I see right away. Even though they have their backs to us.

Tommy and Natalie. And they're looking at a phone.

12
Choices

My head is spinning with all the options.

We could get their £2,000! But we'd have to prove it somehow. Could we stop a passer-by and get them to take a picture on their phone?

We could confront them! That's what River wants to do. I manage to stop him by shaking my head hard and pulling him backwards. Now he looks like he thinks I'm mad.

We could ignore them altogether. Pretend it never happened. But they're cheating! It's not fair!

Maybe it isn't even them? But it's Natalie's blonde ponytail and skinny shoulders all right, not to mention the fuchsia nail varnish.

We could get their £2,000! But Natalie wouldn't be my friend any more.

Would I care that much? That's a lot more money for a trip to New York. And Natalie can be a bit of a snark.

River breaks into my thoughts. "Esther? What are we going to do?"

"Can we stop someone and get them to take a picture?" I suggest.

"What?"

"We could win their money!" I say. "But we need proof, and without a mobile phone ..."

"What? No!" River says. "I'm not spying on them!"

I should have realised that's how he'd feel.

"Sorry," I say. "It's just that they're cheating. Clearly breaking the rules. And it doesn't seem fair ..."

"I'm not spying, no matter how much money's at stake." River is looking at me, puzzled. "I didn't think you were like that."

I'm trying not to feel too upset. But it's a bit much to be told off and at the same time lose your chance to have plenty of money to take Mum and Avi to New York.

"I'm not!" I tell him. "Are you saying I'm greedy? I have a good reason for wanting to win as much money as I can."

River shrugs.

"Seriously!" I say. "Are you so rich that you don't care about money?" He has no answer.

We're halfway up the path. We watch as Natalie and Tommy put the phone away (in Natalie's bag) and walk out of the Manor House exit of the park.

Huh.

"I'm going home," I say. The beautiful day, the great run – it all feels spoiled.

"Look, we need to talk about this." River's frowning. "Why don't you come back to my house?"

"I need to have a shower and get changed," I tell him.

"Come round after, then. We've just moved house – it's a bit of a mess." River gives me the address and leaves me by the entrance to the park. I'm suddenly aware of all the people in the street, and how sweaty and messy I must look. So I run all the way home.

"There you are," Mum says as I come in. "There's another postcard for you from Rosa. And Dad really wants you to Skype."

"I can't," I tell her. "I need to have a shower and then I'm going out."

"But, Esther—" She's interrupted by her ringtone (Elton John). "I'd better get this," she says.

I take the postcard. A picture of Central Park, which looks – I can't lie – a lot smarter than Finsbury Park. The other side is covered with small writing. I'm so happy! I decide to save it until I've had my shower.

The shower feels good. I take my time, drying my hair, choosing what to wear. (I go for my black dress – I like to think it makes me look older, taller and like I might be a very young MP or someone else important and serious and interesting.) I do my make-up. And I twitch to take a selfie and send it to Natalie, but that makes me remember her secret phone and I feel cross all over again.

I mean, why didn't Natalie tell me? Does she think she can't trust me? I bet Shaquilla and

Sophie know. And what's going on with her and Tommy? Normally I'd know every detail by now.

At last. Time for Rosa's postcard.

Hi Essie!

How are you? How's The Disconnect going? How's the cafe, and Mum and Avi?

It's all fine here. Zack is so cute. He can sit up all by himself, and roll over, and he's babbling all the time. It's like he's practising being able to talk. I'm beginning to realise that he won't be a baby for long! I know that sounds silly, but I never really thought beyond the first year. It was such a huge thing – "I'm having a baby!" – that I never really thought about him being a real human. Someone who can talk for himself. His own person.

Anyway, it's all going well with Carlos. I know it was a bit touch and go for a while, but he's really committed to Z, and me, and he wants us to come with him when he goes to San Francisco. Like, to live with him. Wouldn't that be cool? So we're going to have a look, next week. Just to see what it's like. California! Can you imagine?!

Lots and lots and lots of love,
Rosa xxxxxx

13
Info check

On the way to River's house, I stop by the shop that Maura told me about and buy a bunch of postcards. They're nice – all sorts of designs – but I'm too upset to spend much time picking them. I grab some at random and then go into the post office to buy stamps. I stand at the counter to write one (it's got a picture of Buckingham Palace):

What? San Francisco? But I'm going to come and see you in NEW YORK! Now I have to choose between you and Dad. That's not fair, Rosa.

That's if I finish The Disconnect. Otherwise I guess I'll never see you again. Or Dad.

It's not OK when you never see people. It's not the same, talking on a phone or

*sending postcards. It's nothing like the
same. You KNOW that. Why did you have
to go so far away? Why can't you come
home?*

*My friend is cheating. She's breaking
the rules. And I don't know what to do
about it.*

I shove it into the postbox. Then I think some
more and pick another card (a kitten in a plant
pot):

*Actually, Mum and Avi are really worried,
and the cafe is losing money. Someone's
leaving bad reviews on the internet. I
don't know what to do.*

*And my friend who's cheating? I don't
even know if I want her to be my friend
any more. So maybe I should tell on her
and get the money?*

*But River – he's my new friend – he's
really against spying on principle. And
I don't know how I'd prove Natalie's
cheating anyway.*

I wish you were here! I MISS YOU SO MUCH. It's not like missing Dad. He was never here.

I post that one too.

Then I walk to River's house, getting lost twice because how does anyone find their way without GPS? It turns out River lives in a big house up the hill, and I really should have got the W3 bus because it stops next to his street.

I never knew River was rich, I think as I walk up the path to his front door.

The door is opened by a tall white guy with the shiniest hair I've ever seen, and the longest legs. He's holding a tiny baby and he looks a bit harassed.

"Hello?" the guy says.

"I'm Esther – River's friend."

"I'm Jason—"

There's the sound of crying coming from somewhere – but it's not the baby sleeping on his shoulder. "Oh no," Jason says. He thrusts the baby at me. "Can you just ... got to get his sister. River's somewhere about ..."

I freeze. The baby nuzzles against my neck. He's like a tiny version of River, with his light brown skin and his dark curls. I fall instantly in love.

With the baby. Not River. Obviously.

I just stand there, unsure what to do. Then a door opens and a lady comes out who must be River's mum, and she says, "Oh! Who are you?"

"I'm Esther – River's friend," I say again.

She grins and says, "Let me grab Rowan from you," as she scoops the baby into her arms. "This is what happens when I ask for half an hour to do some work. River's just popped out but he'll be back soon. Come with me."

She's so nice. She takes me into their kitchen. "The only decent room," she says. "We only moved in three months ago, and then the twins arrived and, well, it's been a bit chaotic." She puts baby Rowan down in a Moses basket and asks if I go to school with River and if I am doing The Disconnect.

"And how's it going?" River's mum asks.

"Some things are good," I tell her. "But others ... it's kind of difficult." And I find myself talking about what it's like feeling left out of stuff, and how Natalie has been cheating, and how I'm scared that if I tell on her I'll be left out of everything – disconnected for ever. Yet some things are so much better without a phone, and I'm not even sure if I want it back. "And then there's Dad. That's a problem."

But then the tall shiny guy comes in with a screaming baby, saying, "I'm sorry, but I just can't get Gaia to settle, can you?" and River appears at the kitchen door, carrying a shopping bag that he puts on the table.

"Sorry, Esther, come outside in the garden," River says. "Mum, just wait, put it away, can you?"

"Breastfeeding is a normal human activity, River," his mum says, but she waits till we've left the room. The baby stops crying the next second.

The garden is huge and there's a shaded bit at the bottom, with a picnic table where it looks like River's been doing homework, judging by the Maths books spread out there.

"This garden! Wow!" I say.

"It's all Jason," River says. "My stepdad. He's really rich. He sort of insisted we move when he knew they were having twins. It's a bit unnecessary if you ask me. I mean, it's too much for one family. I've been looking into hosting a refugee. Maybe we'll do that."

"That'd be a good idea," I say.

"I know, I keep on telling them," River says. "But they're a bit tired right now, and Mum thinks we need to decorate and stuff. It seems like a lot of fuss to me. I mean, the house is OK as it is, and the babies will only mess it up."

"Do you like having them?" I ask. "The babies, I mean."

He shrugs. "They're cute. But very noisy. And I am not changing nappies for anyone. In fact, they really shouldn't use disposable nappies at all ... I'm surprised at my mum."

River is clearly the sort of person who cares about big stuff. Politics and pollution and the planet. I can imagine how Natalie would roll her eyes and yawn.

But without Natalie being here to judge him, I decide that I'd much rather worry about world affairs and the environment than how many likes I get for a selfie.

"So, what are we going to do?" I ask him.

"About Natalie and Tommy?" River says, and screws up his face. "Er, nothing? I'm not even that friendly with Tommy. He's a bit of an airhead, isn't he?"

"I thought he was your friend."

"Nah," River says. "We played football together a few years back. I haven't really got any friends at that school. Not close friends ... not any more."

I sense that it's better not to ask why.

"Natalie is my friend," I tell him. "But I don't think I can go on being friends with her if she's cheating like this."

"What if you talk to her?" River asks. "See if she'll quit The Disconnect?"

"But I wouldn't like that either. We were doing it together."

"Would it make such a difference? I mean, would you quit if she did?"

I think about it. Just three weeks to go now. I know I can do that. But it'll be much harder without Natalie. She'll be going on about stuff she's seen on her phone, stuff that I'm missing out on, people, memes ...

Memes – I'm actually considering messing up my chances of getting £1,000 because I won't be able to see videos of flying kittens or whatever. *Pull yourself together, Esther.*

"I'm going to talk to Natalie," I decide. "Maybe I can get her to quit. Or stop using the phone."

"What if you can't?" River asks. "What if she wants you to cheat as well?"

"I'm not cheating," I tell him. "I quite like not having a phone."

"I thought it'd be harder than it is," River says. "But I don't like having to wait to find out things."

"You mean, social things?" I ask.

"No, facts. If, say, I want to know the population of China, or the number of polar bears killed by climate change in the last year."

Suddenly, I am desperate to know those things too.

"How can you find out?" I ask him.

"I have to store everything up and look them up on the computer when I get home. But Jason thinks I should go one step further ... give up the internet altogether."

Is he mad?

"How could you do that?" I say. "You wouldn't be able to find out anything!"

"Libraries," he says. "Ringing people up and asking them stuff."

"It'd take for ever." I try to imagine how slow life would be without any internet at all. "It's ... just ... we couldn't *function*."

"I tell you who I *have* been looking up," River says. "Dame Irene Irvine. She's made so much money from mobile phones. Why is she paying us to give them up? And what advice does she need from us?"

River's right. I'd like to find out too.

"So, we should go to a library?" I ask him.

"No, we can use the computer here," River says. "We don't have to give up the internet completely. It was just an idea of Jason's. To take the experiment to the next level."

I'm pretty relieved. We go back into the house, where all is quiet. Both babies are asleep in their baskets and River's mum is bent over her laptop. Jason's flopped out on the sofa and sleeping as soundly as the twins.

River leads me to a side room that is clearly someone's office – there are lots of box files and notebooks and two computers side by side.

"Jason's a journalist," River reminds me, and I hear a note of pride in his voice.

"He's not a restaurant critic, is he?" I ask hopefully.

"No, an investigative reporter." River looks a bit puzzled. Then he says, "Oh! Your cafe."

"Never mind," I say.

"I'll tell him about it. The food was great."

He types "Dame Irene Irvine" into the search engine. (Not Google, I notice, but one I've never heard of. When I ask why, River says, "This one doesn't mine your data.")

At first there are just millions of posts and we don't know where to start. So River adds "teenagers" to his search and "giving up mobile phones".

Nothing obvious. Nothing interesting.

So he adds "experiment".

"Aha!" he says.

There's a report of a conference from 2014 on some website.

"Irvine wants to 'experiment' on teens," it says.

Multi-millionaire Dame Irene Irvine openly admitted that she's planning to create a GENERATION of people addicted to her mobile phones.

She told an industry conference that "it'd be fascinating" to take phones away from youngsters, to "pinpoint" the source of their addiction to technology.

It was crystal clear that her intention was to make sure that new products would be even MORE addictive and ENSLAVE more teens to technology.

"If we can find the outliers, the ones who aren't addicted, we can learn so much," Dame Irene said.

"I'm looking for a school to work with, to test my theories."

Watch out schools! Dame Irene wants to use you to suck even more kids into her grasping claws!

"Oh my God," I say.

"I thought so," River replies. "I thought it must be something like this." He's frowning again. River's got the wildest scowl when he's annoyed about something.

"I'm going to have to quit," he says. "I might go on being disconnected, because I think there are benefits. But I'm quitting The Disconnect. How about you?"

14
Snap cheat

All day Monday at school I monitor Natalie. Will she say or do anything that makes her cheating obvious?

No. Natalie's very good. She manages to be fake-annoyed that Shaquilla's having a party and hadn't consulted her about the guest list. She moans about missing out. She says, "But you'll be sorry when Esther and I have our money."

I'm seething inside. How dare she?

And I'm also wondering *how* Natalie's doing it. Has she created false identities? Is she just a sad lurker, watching everyone else's social media without joining in? Or does everyone know she's cheating – well, Sophie and Shaq anyway – and they're laughing at me behind my back?

I wait until school's over. Natalie and I have English together last period. Then, as we walk out of school, I say to her, "I need to talk to you."

"What?" Natalie asks. "I said I'd meet Tommy."

"Never mind Tommy," I tell her.

"Esther! I said I'd meet him in fifteen minutes. What is it?"

"Why don't you message him to tell him you're going to be late?" I say. "On your brand-new iPhone."

Natalie's perfectly shaped eyebrows shoot up to her fringe.

"My what?" she asks.

"Come off it," I say. "I saw you. We saw you. In the park."

I can see River coming out of the school gates. He's going to tell me that he's done it, I know it. He's quit The Disconnect and got his phone back. And he's going to ask if I've done the same thing. I grab Natalie's arm.

"Come on!" I tell her.

Natalie huffs a sigh and says, "OK, then," like she's doing me a favour. She takes off, marching down the road, not saying a word even when we're down by Finsbury Park station. Then she crosses the busy Seven Sisters Road, under the railway bridge, and weaves in and out of stationary traffic, with me following her.

"Nat! Where are we going?" I ask her.

Natalie reaches the other side of the road, where there's a tall white wall with gorgeous mosaic pictures forming trees and lakes and water lilies. There's also a sign that says "Gillespie Park".

"Ah," I say. "OK." Because our mums used to bring us here when we were small. It always felt like our secret place – the park hidden behind high walls and snaking between railway lines, opening out into trees and meadows and ponds where we'd catch tadpoles. All squashed between the Emirates Stadium and the mosque and all the busy roads and Arsenal tube station. A little bit of green in the city.

We go into the almost hidden entrance and walk along the path by the railway line. It's all fenced off, of course, but it's still about as near as you can get to the line without actually being on a station platform.

"OK," Natalie says. "I cheated. I admit it. But I didn't really cheat. I mean, I haven't used the phone properly. Just to look at stuff. And take pictures and you know … just having a phone … it's useful."

"You are an addict!" I say. "Why not just give up The Disconnect? Get your own phone back?"

"Because I still feel like I'm disconnected! I'm not using it like I normally do. I'm just, you know … there are some useful apps … Twitter …"

"You're not even on Twitter!" I tell her.

"I am." Natalie looks embarrassed. "Murray Myles fandom."

"Oh. Why didn't you say?"

She gives me a sideways look. "I thought you'd laugh at me."

"Oh and why would I do that? Especially when I'm @murraylove?"

Natalie almost falls over. "You what? What the actual?"

"I love the fandom," I tell her.

"I do too," Natalie says. "And I've talked to you on Twitter! Without even knowing it was you! I'm @murraygirl."

And we're laughing out loud, because this is so strange and without The Disconnect maybe we'd never have worked it out.

"We would too," Natalie says when I tell her this. "We'd have had a meet-up at some point – maybe for a concert."

"I don't meet people off the internet! You could have been some pervy lorry driver called Trevor!"

This starts us off again.

"And I'd never have the money for concert tickets," I add.

We've reached the bit of the park that's wider and greener, and there are mums and kids and a lot of trees. And I think about how The Disconnect has been a bit like Gillespie Park for me. A small slither of my life where I can breathe. Where there's silence and time and it's not all rush, rush, chat, chat like the busy streets and railway lines.

I try to explain it to Natalie, but she shakes her head. "Honestly, I can't think of one good thing about The Disconnect. It was Tommy's idea to use spare phones – he's got old ones at home, so we just bought pay-as-you-go SIMs for them. I honestly thought I'd go mad without any kind of smart phone. This way, it's not easy, but I get a little bit of that feeling. You know, the excitement when you're looking to see what's new. What's happening."

"I don't get that feeling," I tell Natalie. "It's more like I feel anxious that I'm missing something. Or someone's been mean about me."

Natalie shakes her head. "You know, sometimes things happen, and people think you're nasty, but you're not really. You get muddled up, or you say something without thinking ..."

"What do you mean?" I ask.

"Your new friend Maura," Natalie says. "I feel ... embarrassed. I think I was one of the people who upset her. But I didn't plan it or anything, it was just one of those things ..."

I wait for her to explain.

"You know how just suddenly there's a joke and everyone joins in, and you don't really know why?" Natalie asks.

"No. Not really," I say. My voice is colder than I expected it to be.

"Well, all I can remember is that somehow it was the thing to do, to laugh at pictures of Maura. And other girls as well. It made us feel grown up. Like, we were laughing at them for being babyish, and that meant we were better than them."

Part of me is desperate to know if I was one of those girls that got laughed at. And part of me wants to walk away and never see Natalie again.

But there's a tiny bit of me that understands what it's like to want to fit in with the crowd.

"It doesn't really feel like bullying if it's online," Natalie finishes. "But when Maura cried, I felt terrible."

"But you didn't do anything about it," I point out. "Like telling her, or saying sorry."

"I felt too embarrassed. And I didn't think she'd want to hear that I remembered."

I take a deep breath and say, "You have to tell her. And you either give Tommy back his phone or I will report you."

"That's OK," Natalie says. "Then you could get my money and give some of it to me!"

"Natalie!"

We've reached the Arsenal station exit of the park, and we step out onto the quiet street. It's so funny to think that these houses once had a huge football stadium right in the middle of them. Now there are flats there, but you can still see the breaks in the terraces where the entrances used to let fans in to see the matches. That's London. Full of secrets and history.

Natalie pulls out her phone. "OK," she says. "I'll give it up."

"Why would you bother?" I burst out. "I wouldn't tell on you. You know that."

"But you wouldn't be my friend any more. I know I've let you down, Esther, but I really don't want to lose you. And I will say sorry to Maura. You just have to help me to do it."

Natalie's crying now and so am I.

"We've been friends forever," she says through her tears. "Sometimes I feel like you're the only person connecting me with the nice girl I used to be, before I turned into Queen Bitch."

I never realised Natalie knew that was what some people called her.

"It's OK," I tell her. "Say sorry to Maura, be her friend, that's all you need to do."

"But what about this stupid phone?" Natalie wails, waving the phone under my nose. I start thinking about how great it'd be to FaceTime Rosa and Dad ... to take pictures and send them ... to watch Murray Myles gifs ... just to be able to find out when the next bus home was coming ...

My hand goes out to take the phone.

And then a moped speeds up and swerves onto the pavement, its driver wearing a balaclava mask. He grabs the phone out of my hand and starts pulling at my school bag. "Oi!" I shout, and try to pull the bag back.

Natalie's screaming, people are running towards us, and then the driver shoves me, hard. I feel my feet leave the ground, and I'm falling – helpless – and the driver's zooming off down the road.

And then I crash to the ground, and the worst searing pain flashes through my foot. Deep, deep inside it I feel something go "snap".

15
Download

I cry all the way to accident and emergency, and
Natalie cries too. The ambulance man tries to
calm us down, saying, "It's only a phone! You can
get another one!" but that just makes us more
hysterical.

Mum meets us at the Whittington Hospital.
"Esther! What happened?" She gives me a hug
and then hugs Natalie too and sends her home in
an Uber.

And then we wait and wait, and I try to
explain why I'm so upset, but I can't get Mum
to understand. Probably because I don't really
understand myself.

"I just don't know what to do!" I cry.

"But if you're so upset about giving up your
phone, then just drop out," Mum says. "It doesn't
really matter." She's distracted, looking at her

messages. "I'll just text Avi, tell him what's happened ..."

"It's not the phone!" I tell her. "I don't care about the phone! It's everything else!"

"Oh, sweetie ..." Mum says. "I didn't realise."

"No, you don't realise, because you're always on *your* phone."

Mum looks shocked. Then she switches her phone off, puts it in her bag and says, "Tell me."

It all rushes out. Natalie. Dame Irene. Maura. The Disconnect. The cafe. And now Rosa saying she's going to live in California.

"I'm never going to see her again!" I say.

Mum hugs me. "It's OK, Esther. We will see Rosa, and Zack – and your dad. It's so much easier than it was when I was in America and my family was here. Auntie Tamsin and I ..."

"You sent postcards, I know," I say.

"We sent postcards," Mum says, "but they were so superficial. All about the good stuff. Nothing about how I felt lonely and homesick, and worried about how your dad would make a living if we came back to the UK. And Tamsin, well, she

told me she was ill, but I had no idea how bad ..."
Her voice wobbles. "She was so brave. It wasn't
until I came home that I realised how sick she
was. Tamsin and I talked more – *really* talked –
in the weeks before she died than we had all our
lives."

"Oh, Mum," I say, and squeeze her hand.

"It doesn't matter *how* you communicate,"
Mum says. "What matters is what you say."

"I don't like to worry anyone," I say. I've only
just realised that.

"Well, I'm happier hearing how you feel than
watching you bottle it all up." Mum kisses my
forehead. "I'm sorry if I'm on my phone too much.
Maybe I should try a dose of The Disconnect too."

"Not all the time," I say. "When the
experiment is over, I think I might try to switch
my phone off one day a week."

"A day of rest," Mum says. "I think that's a
great idea."

Someone comes to call me for my X-ray, and
I have to go and sit on an examination table and
try to angle my foot in different directions. It

really hurts, and I can only hop around on my good foot as I get up and down from the table.

When I come out, Mum is holding her phone, and as soon as I sit down she hands it to me.

"Esther, it's Rosa and your dad," Mum says.

I burst into tears all over again. "I don't want to talk to them! I'm not feeling good!"

"Esther, sweetie," Dad says.

"Essie! How's your foot!" Rosa asks. "What happened?"

"Go away!" I tell them. "Not now! I can't deal with this!"

Mum puts her arm around me.

"She's shaken up," she says.

I can hear Dad's voice, but I'm crying too hard to see him on the screen.

"Esther," he says, and his voice is so full of love that I realise how much I've missed him. Even a distant, far-away Dad-on-the-phone is better than nothing. I realise how mean I've been, disconnecting from him. And how much I want that ticket to New York.

"I'm sorry," I sob. "I didn't break the rules, but now they might think I did. Maybe I won't get the money. I'm sorry."

I can hear them all reassuring me. "It's all right, it's OK." I'm not to worry. Then the doctor calls me, and Mum says she'll have to hang up.

Mum and I go in together and the doctor shows me the tiniest line on the X-ray. It's just under my littlest toe and he says I've broken my fifth metatarsal.

"Common footballer's injury," the doctor tells me. "David Beckham did it. Also Wayne Rooney."

Then there's more waiting, while they fit me with a surgical boot and give me crutches. They tell me I have to use the crutches at all times.

"How long for?" I ask.

"At least a month," the nurse says. "You'll get a letter with an appointment for the fracture clinic."

Goodbye running sessions with River, I think. And goodbye our friendship too, once River realises that I'm carrying on with The Disconnect. Because I am carrying on. I still want that £1,000.

In fact, now I want the money even more than I did before. That's if I *can* still be a part of it – as long as people don't think I'm cheating because the thief took a mobile out of my hand.

*

It's late by the time Mum and I get home. Avi's finished at the cafe and he's made chicken soup "the Persian way" he says. It has dried limes which give it a lemony flavour and meat dumplings which make it into the most comforting meal ever.

And I'm so glad that I have Avi in my life that I cry big fat tears into the soup.

"Hey, hey, does it need more salt?" Avi says gently. "Do you need a paracetamol? Is the foot hurting?"

"Not the foot ... everything else."

"Tell me," Avi says. "My mother always used to say that worries go down better with soup."

"I don't know what to do," I tell him. "When people hear about the robbery, they're going to think I've been cheating on The Disconnect, but I haven't. And we've found out that the woman who challenged us, Dame Irene, she's just exploiting us. She's using us to find out how to get people more addicted to phones."

"Well, you're not going to let yourself be used, are you?" Avi asks me. "So do you want your phone back again?"

I think about it and slowly shake my head.

"I do," I say, "but I want to complete the challenge. I miss my phone, but I'm finding out things about myself without it. I feel more self-confident, and calmer ... most of the time."

"But you miss your dad," Avi says. "And Rosa. And they miss you."

"It's so stupid," I say. "I mean, we can still Skype."

"And your postcards ... and this came today."

Avi hands me a package covered with stamps from New York. I open it up. "Oh! Wow!"

A bundle of postcards falls out. I count them. Twenty.

Ten have been made from photos of Rosa, Zack, Dad and places in New York.

But some are pictures drawn for me by Dad. Like he used to make when I was small. And they tell a story – a man holding a baby, arguing with people in suits, looking very sad on a plane, waiting for a phone to ring.

And on the other side of the postcards, there are loads and loads of words to read.

Some from Dad, some from Rosa.

"Happier?" Avi asks, and I smile. I take another mouthful of soup and things do feel better.

16
Delete and reset

"Come on," I say, "You can do this."

"I can't!" Natalie says. "I said I would, but I'm just too embarrassed."

I lean on my crutches and lead her between the break-time crowds to Maura's corner. Maura's eating an apple and reading a book.

"Hi, Maura," I say.

She looks up and sees Natalie. Her eyes narrow, just a bit, but it makes me certain she knows very well that Natalie was among her bullies.

"Natalie's got something to say, haven't you?" I say, and give Natalie a nudge.

"I just want to say ..." Natalie pauses. "That I've said and done some stupid things in the past, and bullying you was one of them. I'm really sorry. If you ever decide to go back on social media, I've totally got your back."

Maura just looks at her, and for a minute I can't breathe, worrying that she's going to refuse to accept Natalie's apology. Then Maura says, "OK, well, thanks for saying that," and I jump in and ask her what she's reading. We have a slightly awkward conversation about our favourite authors, which warms up a bit when Maura and Natalie discover a shared love for romance stories.

And then River spots me and comes charging over.

"I've done it!" he says. "I've stopped doing The Disconnect. I told Miss Chen that I was taking a stand against manipulation by big businesses. How about you?"

"Err, no," I say as I look at my shoes. "I'm still going on with it."

River's eyebrows go up, and he rubs his nose, and the smile disappears from his face. "Oh," he says. "Shame. Oh well. How did you hurt your foot, by the way?"

"I fell and broke my fifth metatarsal."

"Oh, classic footballing injury," River says. "David Beckham—"

"And Wayne Rooney," I interrupt. "I know. That's what everyone says."

"How did you fall over?" River asks.

I hesitate. And Natalie answers for me.

"We were mugged. A guy on a moped snatched my phone from Esther."

"But you weren't meant to have a phone!" Maura says, open-mouthed.

"I was cheating," Natalie says. "And I'm sorry about that. And I'm going to Miss Chen to confess."

There's a bit of a crowd around us now and I can hear their voices buzzing away. "Natalie … Esther … phone. Phone. Phone." I can only imagine the messages that will be sent about us this afternoon.

But I don't care. Let them say what they want. I gather my crutches together. "Come on," I tell Natalie. "Let's get it over with."

17
Connected

And now we're nearly at half term, and it's the very last day of The Disconnect, and I've done it. I've really done it!

There's a special assembly, with Dame Irene there. We all have to look smart – ties done up with two stripes showing, our blazers on. Everyone files into the hall in silence. Those of us who've managed to complete the challenge sit in the front row – Maura, me and just five others, including Tommy. I'm at the end, surgical boot sticking out in front of me, crutches to the side.

Dame Irene steps up to the microphone. Tells us she's proud of us. Tells us she's looking forward to talking to us, hearing more about our experiences. Says she hears there have been dramas along the way – giving a significant look at my boot – and getting through those is part of what The Disconnect is all about. And she says well done, and can we come up one by one and receive a certificate, a cheque for £1,000 and "most importantly" our phones back.

Ms Mohammed hands Dame Irene a list of names. People start going up.

"Eshe Teferi, Abdul Ibrahim, Lily Brown, Wiktoria Nowak, Maura Lennard ..."

There's a rustling sound behind me, a slight murmur. Ms Mohammed glares in our direction.

"Tommy Olivero, Esther Levin ..."

"Cheat!" yells Natalie, on her feet. For one horrible moment I think her finger is pointing at me. But no – she means Tommy.

"Natalie, sit down at once!" Ms Mohammed says.

But the room erupts in noise and movement, and Natalie keeps on saying "Cheat!"

And then I realise that a lot of people in the room must think that Natalie *is* pointing at me, and I feel like I'm dying inside.

Ms Mohammed goes completely Guantanamo Bay prison guard, shouting at all of us to be quiet and commanding Ms Darcy to march Natalie to the head teacher's office.

And then River stands up.

"It's not Esther that's the cheat," he says, and for a second I think he's going to make it clear that Tommy is the actual villain here. "It's you, Dame Irene. You told a conference in 2014 that you wanted to use people like us to find ways to make us even more addicted to phones than we are!" And River quotes from the article we read on the internet, while Ms Mohammed blows her whistle and tries to shout over him.

"You WILL be quiet! You ARE in trouble."

But River gets all the words out.

And some people cheer, and some boo, and Ms Mohammed looks like she's going to explode. She blows her whistle so hard that even Mr Lamarr is holding his ears.

At last there is silence. Dame Irene says, "I think perhaps, Mr Lamarr, you need to teach your students more about how to assess sources of information. There's a lot of false news flying about nowadays."

Dame Irene pauses, adjusts her pearl earrings. "I wanted to set up The Disconnect because I've been increasingly worried about the direction in which our culture is moving. I believed the mobile phone would liberate people, but it has turned into the biggest social problem of our time."

What about homelessness? I think. *What about knife crime?* But I don't say anything.

"The Disconnect has been a chance to look at this very new form of addiction," Dame Irene continues. "I think the results have been illuminating. So many of you found it impossible to give up your phones – even for a day. I introduced a new element, a few weeks in, to prove another point. I asked you to spy on each other. From that I thought you'd learn how difficult it is to provide proof of cheating, unless you have your camera phone in hand. But also, how much easier it is to spy on others when you have a phone. Privacy is becoming a thing of the past!"

Tommy nudges me. "Do you think we're going to get our money?" he asks in a whisper.

Dame Irene is coming to the end of her speech. "So, today I'm announcing the beginning of a new charity. The Irvine Foundation for the study of phone addiction. And this is what I'd like your help with. Eshe, Abdul, Lily, Wiktoria, Maura ..." she smiles at them, "you are all going to be my advisors. Tommy and Esther, we hope to have your company too, once Mr Lamarr has investigated these allegations of cheating."

I open my mouth to tell Dame Irene that it's all a mix-up, that the phone the mugger took wasn't mine and it's all Tommy's fault, but she's already swept from the stage. And now everyone's filing out, and Ms Mohammed is coming over to us. Her face is always grim, but now it's like a volcano that's about to erupt. I swear there's steam coming out of her nostrils.

"You two, to the head's office," Ms Mohammed says.

"But what about our money?" I ask in a tiny voice.

"Good luck with that!" Ms Mohammed barks.

18
Selfie

It's the Saturday at the end of half term and things at Basabousa are looking up. A journalist came and had lunch, and then wrote about us in the *Evening Standard*. Since then it's getting hard to get a table. Mum and Avi are talking about taking on a sous chef.

I'm helping in the cafe when the door opens and River Jones comes in. *Oh no. What will I do?*

I scuttle off into the kitchen and make Avi take River's order. But when Avi's made it (his special spinach omelette), I have to take it to the table, along with River's mint tea. "You can manage without the crutches just this once," Avi says. "I never had crutches when I broke my foot."

So I limp along to River's table with just the boot.

"Here you go," I say, plonking his food down.

"Esther, I'm really sorry," River says. "I totally believed that article about Dame Irene."

"I know. It was convincing."

"I went home and showed it to Jason," River explains. "He said the guy who runs that website is well known for twisting the facts. I should have realised. I was a total idiot."

"Oh."

"And I was sort of judgemental when you didn't give up The Disconnect when I did. But now I realise that you probably didn't want to say that I was jumping to conclusions from reading that article."

"Oh," I say again. "Well. Not actually—"

"Can we go running together again when your foot is better?" River asks.

I assure him that we can, and then I feel a bit short of things to say and it's suddenly feeling very hot in the cafe.

"I hope it helped when Jason brought his friend here for lunch," River goes on. "His friend who writes restaurant reviews?"

"That was him?" I ask. "It did help, thank you."

"Did you ever get your phone back?" River asks. I explain that I did, because Mum phoned up and complained, but I didn't get the £1,000.

"But that's not fair!" River's outraged, but I'm sort of over it.

"It's not fair, but it's OK," I tell him. "I'm going to try to save up from the tips I get here. We have a lot more customers now. And Mum says she'll chip in so that I can go out to New York before my sister leaves for California."

"But you gave up your phone for six weeks!" River says. "You didn't cheat at all!"

"I learned a lot," I say. "I actually think it was kind of life-changing."

The door opens again and it's the people for the big table in the window. Eight of them. Avi was so happy when that booking came in. I'm showing them to their table, giving out menus, when I realise that Maura is one of them.

"Hey, Esther," Maura says. "I said I'd bring the family."

"I didn't realise you had so much family!" I say.

"Well, some are friends of my parents," she says, "like …"

Maura points towards the woman at the door and I see that puffy white hair. Dame Irene Irvine.

"Oh!" River and I say together.

"Dame Irene is my mum's best friend," Maura says. "They were at school together."

"Why didn't you say?" I ask.

"She swore me to secrecy."

There's a lot of cheek kissing going on, and chatting and looking at menus. Luckily Dame Irene doesn't seem to recognise River or me. Or she has but she's carefully avoiding eye contact.

"But why?" I ask Maura.

"Well, she knew I'd had a hard time and was feeling a bit isolated. So I think she wanted to give other people a chance to think about how much they used their phones and what it meant to them. And I have made a lot of new friends. So ... it's all good really."

It's all good except for my missing £1,000, I think.

But then I think about all the things I got from The Disconnect. Better grades. New friends. More confidence. A better friendship with Natalie.

Time for reading. A new appreciation of my dad, my family here and there. Maybe all that was worth doing without the reward. New York will have to wait.

Avi's here to take the order. He leans down to speak to Maura and River. "You guys, make sure you come back here at five o'clock. We're going to have a small celebration for Esther's birthday."

"My birthday isn't until Tuesday!" I say.

But Avi winks and says, "Tuesday's for school. Let's celebrate while you're on holiday."

*

I don't think Maura and River will really come back at five, but they both do. And Natalie, Shaquilla and Sophie come too. Natalie's invited a few more people, and River's called some of the Disconnect kids, and I'm sitting in the middle of a crowd of friends.

Someone takes a picture, and I don't worry at all about them putting it on social media. If I look bad, so what? I won't be looking at any of the snarky comments. I'm never going to measure my worth in likes again.

"I've decided to have one day a week completely phone-free," I tell everyone. "And if I feel my phone is taking over my life again, I'll do a mini Disconnect for a week or so. I mean, there are lots of good things about having a phone. It's just keeping it all in balance."

As I speak, my phone buzzes. Rosa! She's calling me. "Look up," she says when I answer the call. "Look at the door."

"You what?" I say, but I look. At the door ... there's a girl with long curly hair and a baby.

I gasp – could it be? But there she is. My sister, with little Zack in her arms, all the way from New York.

I can't run across the room – stupid boot and crutches – but Rosa runs to me. And we're laughing and crying and hugging and—

"Hey, Essie," a voice says. "I'm here too."

And it's really him. My dad. In the flesh, in London.

"I've got news," Dad says, after we've hugged so tight that I think my ribs might break. "I've got a job. In London. A show in the West End. My agent's sorting the details, but I'm going to be here for a while. I can hardly believe it. We can just hang out. We can be normal for once."

"Oh well," I say. "What's normal?"

I'm so happy, I feel like I'm going to burst.

I grab my phone.

"Dad, Rosa, let me hold Zack ..."

It's time to take a selfie.

Acknowledgements

Thanks to Phoebe and Judah,
my digital natives.